Diary of an Adirondack Faerie

By,

Lovelyn

(With some small encouragement from)

Derek Todd Fisher

I0739929

The Hollow Thing

Moon and Stars

I have never kept a diary before and am not sure why I am starting now, except that Percy thought it might be fun. Percy is a porcupine. Actually I am not even sure that Percy is her name, but I think it is so much fun to say, Percy the porcupine, Ha Ha! and she doesn't mind so I call her that.

I don't really know how to keep a diary, so I will keep it as if I am writing to a friend, but I don't think a friend will read it. I don't think that they are supposed to since it is a diary.

But that is how I will keep it.

Um, Hi, my name is Lovelyn. Oh, I guess I didn't need to write "um".

Well anyway I am Lovelyn and I live here. I don't know how I came to be here, but, this is where I am, so this is where I'll be.

It is very pretty here, so I fit in well. I must admit that I am quite fetching, even through the eyes of Faerie.

There is quick water here that sings and speaks, and still water that thinks deep and pensive thoughts. Many trees to laugh and dance with when the wind comes to play.

And of course all of the animals
and birds and insects.

It is a good place to be.

There is, however, a very strange growth
of some kind. At first the animals and I
thought that it was a type of tree, but the
trees said that it was not.

When we went to look closer we found
it to be hollow and it seemed unnatural to
me, all pointy and misshapen.

Everything was so straight, or so we thought until one of the squirrels dropped a beechnut on the hard ground inside the hollow thing and it rolled away.

And except for some bats that lived in the top, nothing lived there, so the mice thought they might like it and they moved right in. I didn't like it in there because I couldn't see the sun and sky.

Then, after mushroom moon and mushroom moon, another animal moved into the hollow thing.

At first we thought maybe it was a type of Packrat because it kept stuffing more and more things into the hollow thing and we thought that would be good, because a Packrat would get along with the mice who lived there.

But the animal was too big and ugly to be a Packrat.

Marvin the marten, I don't know if that's his name either, but it's fun to say too. "Marvin the marten", I just love that!

Anyway, Marvin the marten, (Ha!) said that the animal thing looked like me a little. Not as graceful or pretty of course, but a similar design.

No wings though. I love my wings. If you don't have them it is hard to describe how amazing they feel.

Anyway, this animal moved in and
after moon and stars and grey with water and
sun and sky and moon and stars, we heard
strange screechy noises and lots of running
and jumping noises in the hollow thing.
We figured that the screechy noises all
came from the animal thing and
we never saw the mice again.
So I guess it ate them.

Lovelyn

Strange Ice

Black with Water

Hi, Lovelyn again, but I guess
you know that.

We have been having big discussions
about the hollow thing and the animal
thing that lives there and probably
ate the mice.

It is all very strange to us. During
moon and stars or black with water, the
hollow thing glows through holes
in the sides of it.

But they are not really holes, we found that out. They look like holes, but there is something that stops them from being holes that looks like very clear ice, but it doesn't melt.

Montrose the moth, Ha Ha! Montrose the moth, I think that is so fun. But Montrose the moth doesn't think so, so I can't call him that. He gets very mad and says, "Miss Lovelyn, my name is NOT Montrose and never will be. My name is Reginald, and a very proper name it is indeed!!"

Montrose the moth is always so proper. (Ha! I called him Montrose again. Oh I don't care, he can't read anyway.)

Well, Reginald, la ti da, tried to melt the clear ice with his wings. He kept flapping and flapping against it until he couldn't flap anymore. All of his friends kept trying too, but the stuff never melted.

I painted some very elaborate and very pretty designs on the stuff that some animal named Jack got all the credit for. But that's alright, I had a wonderful time painting. My painting melted but the clear stuff didn't. I still don't think that it is ice.

Montrose the moth, (I'm going to call him that anyway, Ha!), said that while he was trying to melt the stuff he felt like it was very thin and that if only he were a bit heavier, he thought he could fly right through it.

Flicka Flicka Flicka, isn't that a funny name? Flicka Flicka Flicka, I can say that and laugh so hard I fall over. But that is what she calls herself so that is what she is.

Anyway, Flicka Flicka Flicka, who, by the way is a bit ditsy but much more fun than REG-I-NALD, said she thought that she would try to fly through the ice that doesn't melt and then fly out through another hole in the hollow thing.

We all wanted to watch to see if

she could do it. I had my doubts, but Montrose the moth, (Reginald if you please), said he was "Certain that the experiment would prove a success."

He talks funny like that.

So Flicka Flicka Flicka started to fly up and away so she could get a good run at the hole with the strange ice over it. She got up pretty high, and then down she came and pretty fast too!!

We all watched, except for one of the baby chipmunks who hid his head under his mother's belly.

And WHAM!!!

Flicka Flicka Flicka smacked into the ice with a really loud B A M! and bounced off. Then she just kind of hung there in midair like she was floating and her eyes kept looking all different directions at once, but not looking at anything at all really.

Then she just started flying crazy like a butterfly in a playful wind.

Actually butterflies don't need a playful wind to fly crazy.

They are so funny, I don't know how they ever get to where they want to go.

But then, who knows if they ever really want to get anywhere specific anyway. Maybe they're just glad to have gotten anywhere at all.

Oh, back to Flicka Flicka Flicka.

She flew around like that for a while, bouncing off trees and then the ground, and then a tree again.

She finally stopped when she landed in the quick water. I guess that kind of woke her up or something because Flicka Flicka Flicka yelled,

"WOW! That hurt!!"

Then she stumbled up the hill and sat down next to the chipmunks.

I was going to go, but Montrose the moth just walked over to Flicka Flicka Flicka (I still think that is such a fun name), anyway, Reg-I-nald I mean, walked over and puffed up his little moth fuzz, squeezed Flicka Flicka Flicka's wing and said,

"Nope, not heavy enough. We need one, somewhat thicker." (See how funny he talks?) And he looked over at Periwinkle the partridge.

Isn't that a funny name? Periwinkle, Ha Ha!

Well, somehow Montrose the moth

(I'm still going to call him that. Who ever heard of a moth named Reginald anyway!) Montrose the moth talked Periwinkle the partridge into trying to fly though the ice that doesn't melt, even though we just saw Flicka Flicka Flicka ricochet off and fly around like a lost bat.

"But this time," said Montrose the moth, like he knew what he was talking about, "This time try one of the smaller holes up high.

Being closer to the sun, there is a great likelihood that it will be much softer and more easily breached."

So up goes Periwinkle the partridge. She could fly very fast with her short wings.

I'm glad I don't have short wings, not very becoming, do you think?

She was going very fast by the time she got to the hole with the strange ice on it and the baby chipmunk hid it's head again.

He looked so cute doing that I just wanted to hug him!

But then SMASH!!! There went Periwinkle the partridge right through the ice!

Montrose the moth yelled, "Ah Ha!! I knew it could be accomplished thus!!" (Funny huh?)

Then it was very silent and we all watched for Periwinkle the partridge to come out again, but she didn't.

The animal thing that lives in the hollow thing stuck it's head out of the hole and we never saw Periwinkle the partridge again.

So it probably ate her.

Lovelyn

The Otters

Sun and Sky

Hi, me again, Lovelyn.
Lovelyn Lovelyn Lovelyn!! Ha Ha!
I just love that name. Such a perfect name
for me don't you think?
Lovelyn Lovelyn Lovelyn, Lala
Lala La!!

It is so fun here, we play all the time.
You should have seen the Otters on the
deep water. They are so mischievous, Ha
Ha! I love that about them.

The Geese don't though.

But it was so funny to see I couldn't
stop laughing.

I do feel a little sorry for the geese
though. They fly such a long way and just
want to eat and rest and the
Otters won't let them!

I'll tell you what the Otters did.

The deep water gets ice on it, real ice that
melts, not like the clear ice on the hollow
thing. And sometimes when the deep water
has ice mostly all over it, but there is still
some that sees the sky, the Geese come
to rest and eat.

That is when the Otters play tricks on them.

Otto the otter and Octavious the otter, ha ha! How is that for some fun names! I can call the Otters anything I like, they think it is very funny. They think almost anything is funny.

Anyway, Otto the otter and Octavious the otter, came over to me and said,

"Miss Lovelyn," everybody calls me Miss Lovelyn. I don't know why, but that is what they do so that is what I am.

They said, "Miss Lovelyn, come out to the deep water and watch this, we have the best trick to play on the Geese!!"

Well I almost couldn't tell what Otto the otter and Octavious the otter were saying they were laughing so hard. But I got the idea and went with them.

Otters are so crazy you can't help but love them.

All the Geese were on the ice by the deep water that could see the sky, just where the Otters wanted them.

One Goose, Gethura the goose, oh, I just had to call her a pretty name. Of course I don't know her real name and after what the Otters did I bet she forgot her real name anyway.

Gethura the goose, it is a pretty name, was very close to the deep water, stretching her neck out over it.

I don't know if she was looking for food or watching her reflection, but whatever she was doing she didn't see Otto the otter and Octavious the otter slip into the deep water.

I watched with Faerie sight and saw everything.

The Otters swam under the ice until they were right beneath the Geese and Otto plucked a plant, Haa Haa!

Well he plucked a plant with lots of seeds on the end and held it so it kept waving out from under the ice right where Gethura was looking.

Oh! Her eyes got big! And I think she grinned, which is hard to do when you have a bill.

She leaned way over to get the seeds and

WHOOSH!!!

Out jumped Octavious right next to her!!

Her eyes got really big then and rolled back in her little head. Her wings started flapping like crazy and her poor little feet were a blur, but she was on ice and not getting anywhere.

I think she was trying to honk, but after that first really high pitched squeal when Octavious showed up, all that was coming out were little wheezing noises like she was gasping for breath.

I was laughing so hard I almost fell down! I was bent in the middle and couldn't straighten up at all!

Otto the otter and Octavious the otter were both back under the ice and laughing so hard I could feel them banging their little Otter heads on it and that made me laugh even harder. Haaa Haaaaa!!!!!

The other Geese wanted to know what had happened to poor Gethura the goose, so they gathered close to where she had passed out from fright.

After Gethura the goose lay there for a while, with all the other Geese crowding in on her and making little cooing sounds, Gethura the goose started to twitch a little and in a minute she was full awake and sat bolt upright with a loud HONK!

The other Geese jumped back a bit and started honking at her all at once.

I suppose trying to find out what had happened.

Gethura the goose looked like she didn't even know that they were there.

I could see, now that I could breathe again, that Otto and Octavious the otters, (Ha Ha! they are so funny), had stopped banging their heads and were in the deep water again. I saw their cute little Otter noses just sticking up so they could breathe.

But they were watching the Geese.

Gethura the goose looked like she just couldn't believe that anything could possibly have come out of the deep water like that.

So she got up and waddled over to the edge of the ice like nothing had happened because it couldn't have happened.

All the other Geese must have agreed with this because they all crowded around her very close to watch her.

Gethura the goose put one foot on the edge of the ice, so her one toe was in the deep water and she put all of her weight on that foot and stretched her neck way out to get a better look.

All of the other Geese kind of
leaned with her.

And just when Gethura the goose
was satisfied that nothing had happened,
something grabbed her toe and
up came Otto!!!

I didn't know Geese could do back flips,
but Gethura the goose sure did one. I
had never heard a bunch of Geese all
scream at once before either, it is quite loud,
but not so loud to hide
the Otters' laughter.
I could hardly
stand it, I was
rolling around on the ground
kicking I was laughing so hard.

I could barely see through the tears
when some of the Geese started dropping out
of terrified shock into sheer panic.

The panicking ones seemed to be getting
pretty good traction on the backs, heads and
beaks of the ones still in shock.

It looked like white with wind, there were
so many feathers loose in the air.

And the sound was so funny!

I could hear a lot of started honks that
turned into muffled hhmmpphhhs Haa!!!

I don't think poor Gethura the goose
will ever be the same.

Otto the otter and Octavious the otter
were trying to climb a bank to get out of

the deep water, but they kept laughing and falling back in with a splash that startled the Geese, who were all staggering around with really wide eyes.

I almost had to crawl back home because I couldn't stop laughing at all. I finally did kind of stop though, and at moon and stars I went to check on the Geese.

They were huddled far from the deep water and looked very nervous.

I covered them with Faerie light so they would feel loved and warm and not afraid anymore, but I don't know if they will be back again.

I could still hear the Otters laughing.

Lovelyn

Roscoe The Raccoon

Black with Water and Sky Bright

Hello whoever you are, I hope
you feel fun inside!
Lovelyn again, who else?
The animal thing that lives in the hollow
thing is a very strange animal indeed.
I was talking with Mainard the moose,
Mainard was not my first choice to call
him, but he got a bit upset, in his, kind of
Moose way when I called him
Mallard the moose.

I said, "Hello there Mallard the moose, how is the quick water feeling?"

I thought he should know, he was standing in it.

And he said, "Oh, the quick water is feeling very wel..."

Then he stopped and thought the way Moose do and he said.

"Miss Lovelyn," (I told you everybody calls me Miss Lovelyn) "My name is not Mallard. That is the name of a Duck I think."

And I said, "But it is such a fun name, can't I call you Mallard the moose?"

"No," he said, "I don't want to be called
after a Duck."

"Well you're in the water." I said.

"But I'm not a Duck!" He said,
"And Mallard is a Duck's name."

"Well I don't know the name of every
Duck around!" I said.

We went round and round like that
for a while and I finally just had to call
him Mainard the moose
to make him happy.

OOOHH!!!

Moose can be so obstinate!!

Anyway, Mainard the moose, (not the
best name, but kind of fun), said that the

Deer were very happy and friendly with animal thing, even though they had never actually spoken to it.

But they said the animal thing had worked very hard digging and clearing and putting food in the ground to grow just for them.

Mainard the moose asked the Deer how they knew the food was for them. The Deer said that the animal thing wrapped the place where the food was with magic shiny vines that the Rabbits couldn't chew through or dig under, so who else could the food be for?

That was pretty smart I thought.

And all of the food was just the favorite

things Deer love to eat.

So that made sense too.

The only thing is that when the Deer are around, the animal thing stands by the holes with the strange ice and shows its teeth a lot. So it probably wants to eat them.

Well, Roscoe the raccoon, Ha Ha! Roscoe, what a perfect name for a Raccoon!

I can call him that too because he doesn't really listen to what I say anyway.

Raccoons don't listen too much to what anybody says. Otters are crazy in a really fun way, but Raccoons are just nuts!

I saw Raccoons playing near the deep water, they were really funny to watch!

Haha!

They kept falling into and pushing each other into the deep water.

The Raccoon that got pushed into the deep water would get mad and run, plowing into the other Raccoons knocking them down, until one of the Raccoons yelled danger and they all ran up a tree.

But the branch they got on wasn't big enough for all of them.

So one of them pushed another off the branch and he fell into the bushes and got mad and ran back up the tree and pushed another raccoon off and he fell into the bushes and got mad and ran back up the tree and pushed another raccoon off and he fell into the bushes and got mad and it just got worse from there until it looked like the tree was juggling.

It was really funny Haa Haa!!!

Then they all fell into the bushes at once and started wrestling around until they remembered the danger and they all stopped at once and it was very still.

Then WHOOSH!!!

They all rushed up the tree at once like a quick wind!!

But this time there was room on the branch. So I guess something ate one.

See, nuts.

Anyway, Roscoe the raccoon (Ha,
Roscoe) thought that if the animal thing
liked the Deer so much,
it would just love him.

I don't know why though. I am much
more lovely than he is, I am sparkly and
light and my wings are sooo pretty. But
I don't think any animal would like me
more than they like any other animal, even
though I am not really
an animal anyway.

Maybe the animal thing wrapped the
magic vine around the food because it doesn't
want to eat the rabbits.

But like I said,
you can never tell with Raccoons.

So Roscoe the raccoon walked up to the hollow thing where the animal thing goes in and out and banged on the thing that covers the hole.

The animal thing uncovered the hole, saw Roscoe the raccoon standing there and screeched like it did when it probably ate the mice and covered the hole again really quickly.

Roscoe the raccoon, (that is such a great name for him) anyway he was stunned, no animal had ever screeched at him like that before.

A Bear rolled him down a hill once

and that was really funny! Haa Haa!!
But he'd never been screeched at.
Roscoe the raccoon said it hurt his little
raccoon feelings too.
He told me that all he wanted to do
was just to go into the hollow thing and eat
everything he could find that he could eat.
"What's wrong with that?"
He asked me.
Just like I said, nuts huh?

Lovelyn.

Filbert The Flying Squirrel

Sun and White

Hello again, why are you reading my diary? Haahaa!!

If you are reading this you are meant to be and so you are!

The wind and trees are so much fun!

The wind was dancing with the trees and the trees were bending far over and standing again and bending the other way and the wind would swirl around so much!

I flew to the top of a tall tree and

rode the branches in the wind.

I just love that!

I was very surprised to see Filbert the flying squirrel sail past. Haa Haa!! Filbert the flying squirrel makes me laugh!

He is much more round than most flying squirrels so he flies about like a rock!

I asked him how he got so round and he told me that it had to do with the hollow thing and the other flying squirrels that went into it and never come out. Naturally Filbert the flying squirrel thought the animal thing ate them.

You would think that Filbert the flying squirrel wouldn't be so curious, especially since the other squirrels probably got eaten, but squirrels are very curious.

Almost as curious as worms.

You wouldn't think that worms would be curious at all, but they are. They are very curious. Why do you think worms eat dirt? YUCK!! It's not because they like it, it is because they are curious to know if they ever will.

Anyway, Filbert the flying squirrel, (Ha! Filbert), just had to know what was so interesting in the hollow thing that the other flying squirrels had to see it.

So in he went.

Filbert the flying squirrel told me he followed the scent of the other flying squirrels to find his way and he ended up in the hollow thing at what looked like a smooth tree, with no branches and strange smooth black bark and it came out of some kind of mushroom or something.

But, that is where the trail went and so that is where he followed.

Well the strange tree was very slippery and down went Filbert the flying squirrel like a stone. (Remember I said that? Ha Ha!)

He said he bonked his little squirrel head on the white mushroom thing and it was a really hard mushroom.

Filbert the flying squirrel, la la la, got knocked out.

When he started to wake up it was moon and stars and he heard a funny voice laughing, he said.

"Well, you did get bonked on the head." I said.

And he said, "NO, it was a _real voice_."

Filbert the flying squirrel said that it was one of the mice that we thought had gotten eaten, but the mouse was really round and tubby. The mouse waddled over and looked at Filbert the flying squirrel and said he was lucky the hole was covered.

Filbert asked, "what hole?"

And the mouse said, "The hole in the mushroom thing when the other squirrels came down the tree and bonked their heads the hole in the mushroom wasn't covered and the squirrels fell in the hole and drowned because there is water in the hole and then the animal thing came in and took them away and probably ate them."

Mice are so funny, they talk really fast, Ha Ha! I wish I could have heard the mouse tell the story, but Filbert the flying squirrel did a fine job too.

Filbert asked the mouse how he got so round and the mouse said…well the mouse told a really long story, but Filbert said the point of it was that there is plenty of good food in the hollow thing and the animal thing hasn't tried to eat them once, but it makes funny noises at them when it sees them.

Sometimes, the mouse said, they jump out just to hear the funny noises, Haa Haa!! But mostly they stay hidden.

So the mouse showed Filbert the flying squirrel, (who is now mostly Filbert the walking squirrel, and I'll have to change his name), anyway, the mouse showed him the food and Filbert got just as round and tubby as the mice

And now he doesn't fly so good.

Lovelyn

Brimley The Bear

Dark with Water

Moose are just weird, don't you think?
Sometimes a Moose will just stare
at nothing from Sun and Sky until
Moon and Stars and hardly move. Like
they had been covered with Pixie dust or
something, but they haven't. And don't even
try to talk to them when they are like that,
they get very startled and then
they can get just mean.
But they never remember that.

I don't think I'll ever understand Moose. Bears on the other hand, they are so cuddly and sweet!! Ha Ha!! I just love Bears. They just go around doing... well, whatever they do, always friendly and helpful. I love Bears.

I love Moose too.

Moose are pretty funny. They eat with their head under water and when they remember they have to breathe and come up for air, their head is covered with water plants and they look like Bog Monsters!! Ha Ha!

Moose are funny, but they are weird.

One of my favorite Bears is Brimley the bear. I just love that name! Brimley, it sounds so sophisticated, don't you think?

Brimley the bear!

And Brimley the bear is such a sweet Bear I just had to call him a fun name like that. And he doesn't mind, he just says, "Miss Lovelyn, you call me whatever pleases you. It always makes me smile the way you name things." And then he gives me a Bear hug. Those are so nice I think, cuddly and sweet.

But it is good I'm a Faerie so I don't get smushed sometimes. Brimley the bear is very strong.

He is not the Bear that rolled Roscoe the Raccoon down the hill though, if you were wondering. That was a different Bear, a Bear named Billy the bear. He is kind of a plain Bear so I call him that.

Billy the bear...that is not such a fun name, I think I'll have to change that.

Anyway Billy the bear (which I will change), is a sweet Bear too, he is just not very tolerant of Raccoons.

He doesn't hurt them, he just rolls them down a hill. Ha Ha!! That is really funny!!

Have you ever seen a dizzy Raccoon stumbling around after being rolled down a hill by a Bear and wondering what he did to deserve it?

Haaa Haaa!!! When maybe he just went to the Bears favorite honey tree and started chasing off the bees just for fun.

Raccoons are nuts.

Anyway, back to Brimley the bear. (He is so sweet.)

Well, Brimley the bear said that he had heard about the other animals getting food from the animal thing that lives in the hollow thing and he wanted to try it too.

Bears will not turn down food...ever.

Brimley the bear told me he walked around and around the hollow thing looking for something he would like to eat but he didn't find anything. But then he noticed that there were things that looked like some kind of puffball just outside of one of the covered holes that the animal thing goes into. But much bigger than puffballs and dark and wrinkled and the scent was not the same.

He said they kind of smelled like they might be food though, so Brimley the bear grabbed one and took a bite.

Brimley the bear (A very good name.) said that the outside was stretchy and slick, like eating a frog but it didn't taste like a frog. Actually, he said, it didn't taste like anything at all really.

But the inside had all kinds of different tastes and he spread everything out so he could smell it better and know what to eat.

Then the animal thing came out of the covered hole.

Brimley the bear was a little startled, but being so sweet he wanted to be friendly, so he stood up. He said the animal thing just made its eyes bigger and stared at him.

And the animal thing just kept staring and Brimley the bear was getting a little nervous. He had seen that look before. Then the animal thing started waving it's paws and making loud noises and Brimley the bear thought it would be best to run away.

And now he thinks the animal thing might be some kind of Moose.

Lovelyn

Buckhannon The Buck

Black with Stars

Oh the stars are so pretty. Sparkly like me!! Haha!!

I don't know where they came from or how they got to be where they are, but that is where they are so that is where they'll be.

Remember Percy the porcupine? (Cute name don't you think?) She wanted me to write this Diary. I am glad she did, I think it's funny! Ha!

Anyway, Percy the porcupine came to me and told me a story to put in the Diary.

She is so sweet and shy, she talks so soft and gentle I just want to kiss her. But I can only kiss her on the very end of her nose though. Haa Haa!!

Anyway she told me about what happened with Buckhannon the buck. Ha!! Buckhannon the buck, now that is a fun name! He really likes it too, so I can call him that!

Well Percy the porcupine told me about Buckhannon the buck and the animal thing that lives in the hollow thing.

Buckhannon the buck was eating the deer food that the animal thing (which Brimley the bear thinks is some kind of Moose, but I don't) put in the ground and he heard a noise, like footsteps.

Then the animal thing came from behind the hollow thing and just stopped and stared at him and showed its teeth.

So naturally Buckhannon the buck thought the animal thing wanted to eat him so he started to back away. Because even though the animal thing is kind of small and ugly, if it is some kind of Moose (which I doubt) it is probably crazy.

But then the animal thing started making strange noises at him. Not the screechy noises like when it sees the mice, but more like maybe it was trying to talk, he said.

So Buckhannon the buck got close to the trees so he could hide if he had to.

But he told Percy the porcupine that the animal thing just went to the place where the deer food is and started taking the food, but not eating any of it and it still kept making strange noises at him.

Then Buckhannon the buck (I love that name. Ha Ha!) said the animal thing just turned and walked away with the food. It didn't even try to chase him, like

the Coyotes did when he was small, before he was Buckhannon the buck.

The Coyotes couldn't catch Fane the fawn, (that is a really fun name for a fawn!) and they would get very mad and yell like…well, like Coyotes.

But the Coyotes don't chase Buckhannon the buck because he has pointy branches on his head.

He said the animal thing just went into the hollow thing again and didn't come back.

Weird don't you think?

Percy the porcupine said maybe it is some kind of Moose. But I still don't think so.

Lovelyn

Rippley The Raccoon

Black with Changing Stars

I love it when the stars change!!
Mmm, don't you love it?
Frogs don't though, so they hide in the
ground and sleep until it's over.
So do the bears.
Sometimes when I want to see Brinley
the Bear, I go to where he is sleeping and
curl up with him and step into his dreams.
Ha Ha!!
He says, "Hello Miss Lovelyn." (I
still don't know why I'm called

<u>Miss Lovelyn</u>. But that is what I'm called so that is what I am.)

And I say, "Hello Brimley the bear."

And Brimley the bear says, "Have the stars stopped changing? Is it time to eat?"

And I say, "Not yet, (unless it is of course), I just wanted to see you."

And he says, "Can you make a honey tree in my dream?"

And of course I do.

I just love Brimley the bear.

Do you know why the sky gets covered when the stars are changing? Ha! I do!

Because if the stars didn't go through the cover they would be going too fast to catch on your tongue! Haa Haa!!

Remember I said that raccoons are nuts? Well they are, but there is a raccoon named Rippley the raccoon who is not as nuts as most raccoons.

Rippley the raccoon, Ha Ha!! That is a good name, but if I call him that I have to call him that really loud because Rippley the raccoon doesn't hear too well.

He is really slow and quiet.

I don't think Rippley the raccoon has ever even been rolled down a hill by a bear.

But the animal thing that lives in the hollow thing got very upset with Rippley the raccoon. I don't know why though.

Rippley the raccoon had gone to the quick water to drink and eat and then wanted to sleep in his favorite hollow tree. (Raccoons love hollow trees).

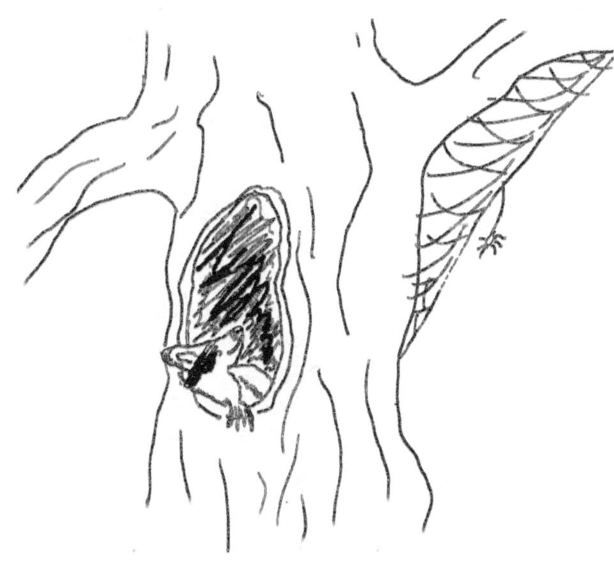

So Rippley waddled up the hill from the quick water and was passing by the hollow thing to get to his sleeping tree, when the animal thing came charging out of the hollow thing screeching like a mad Possum!

Possums are so funny, I don't even have to name them for them to make me laugh. If you just see one you can't help but at least giggle. And possums don't mind if you laugh, they think they look funny too.

But don't get them mad!!

Possums make very odd noises when they get mad and they have sharp teeth!! I have never made one mad, but I've seen them get mad.

I saw one get mad at a weasel once. That weasel ran so fast! Haa Haa!!

Anyway, the animal thing made noises

like a mad possum and showed its teeth too
and chased poor Rippley the raccoon
up a tree.

Poor Rippley, he didn't know what he
did. So he stayed up in the tree for a while.

Then the animal thing went back into
the hollow thing and Rippley the raccoon,
(quite a good name for a raccoon, don't you
think?) came out of the tree and started for
his sleeping tree.

But then the animal thing came after
him again and chased him back up the tree.
And it stood by the tree shaking its paws
and screeching.

I know why the mice jump out at it, the
animal thing looks really funny doing that.

Ha Ha!!

Anyway, the animal thing didn't try
to climb the tree, it just screeched and went
back into the hollow thing.

Then Ripley the raccoon stayed
in the tree for a long
time and came down in
moon and stars and
snuck to his
favorite hollow tree
to sleep.

Rippley the raccoon,
(Ha! Rippley!), said he didn't know why
the animal thing was so mad at him.

But I think the animal thing probably
wanted to eat him.

Lovelyn

Hello whoever you are! I hope you are having a smiling day! I am, Ha! Ha!

Winston the Weasel, Haa! Winston the Weasel! That is a great name for a weasel, don't you think? And I can call him that because mostly he doesn't remember his own name anyway.

Winston the Weasel runs very fast, but he doesn't turn too good so he is always bonking his little weasel head into things and that makes him forget.

He did remember a funny story that he told me, about what happened when he went into the hollow thing though.

I asked Winston the Weasel, (Ha! Winston the Weasel, that is fun to say!) Anyway, I asked him why he wanted to go into the hollow thing. Mostly everything that goes in gets eaten by the animal thing we think.

And he said, "Remember what that squirrel said? What's his name again? Philip? No, not Philip, Flippy? No, that'd be silly, um..."

"Filbert the Flying Squirrel?" I said. (I always smile when I say that).

"No, no, not Filbert. Oh wait, yes, Filastean!"

"Filbert."

"Yes, Filbert!"

I asked what Filbert the Flying Squirrel had said and Winston the Weasel said he didn't really remember, but whatever it was, that's why he went into the hollow thing. Ha Ha! He is so cute.

Anyway, Winston the Weasel said that when he was inside the hollow thing it was warm and cozy and he thought that if the mice could live there maybe he could too.

So he started looking for a good place.

He said he didn't see the animal thing

anywhere and walked out into the middle of the hard ground inside the hollow thing. Then he said the hard ground got fuzzy like the back of a Vole, but not as soft. He said the fuzzy stuff covered the hard ground and was flat, not round like the back of a Vole.

Voles are so funny! Haa! They push their little noses through the ground and make long holes to crawl through and then just pop up and scare the birds. Haa Haa!!

And they think a lot too. They can think almost as much as the deep water sometimes. And that makes sense, because what else is there to do when they're pushing around in the ground?

I watched with Faerie sight and saw a Vole smack into a big rock! Ha! He tried to go this way and that way but it was a really big rock!

So he just sat there in the ground thinking about it from Sun and Sky until Moon and Stars.

He might still be there too. The wind called and I went to play. You can have good talks with Voles sometimes.

Anyway, Winston the Weasel, (who doesn't think deep thoughts and if he did he would probably forget them anyway), walked out on the fuzzy ground. He said it tickled his paws and he stared laughing.

Ha Ha! Have you ever heard a weasel laugh? That is really funny to hear!

Then he heard something coming and he thought it might be the animal thing, so he ran and hid behind a big black rock, (or something he thought might be a rock), but it was hot and there was a tree growing out of the top of it that bent and went out the side of the hollow thing.

Winston the Weasel thought he might like to live behind the hot rock because it was nice and warm and he thought it would be a good place to sleep.

He peaked around the side of it and he saw the animal thing and when the animal thing saw him, it started making the funny

screeching noises like it does when
it sees the mice.

Winston the Weasel said that the animal thing was holding some kind of long flat stick in its paws and started banging it on the ground.

So he hid behind the hot rock again.

While he was hiding he was trying to think of what kind of animal the animal thing might be, but he didn't remember ever seeing any animal like that before.

But remember I said he forgets a lot?

Well, Winston the Weasel (Ha! I still laugh when I say that!), well he thought he should take another look. So he walked around the hot rock thing and the animal thing saw him again and started jumping up and down and banging the stick and screeching again.

Winston said he just stared at the animal thing like it was crazy, which it probably is, but I still don't think it's a moose.

Then Winston the Weasel said he ran and hid under some kind of log. But the log was held up off the ground so he could get under it. He said he stayed under the log for a long time, waiting for the animal thing to leave. But the animal thing walked over and sat on the log and the bottom of the log sagged way down.

I guess the animal thing was pretty heavy. It must have been putting on fat to hibernate.

Well, Winston the Weasel didn't want to get squished so he ran out from under the log and the animal thing jumped up and screeched again and chased poor Winston off the fuzzy ground and onto the hard slippery ground and Winston couldn't turn and he bonked his little Weasel head. But he found the hole he had gotten into the hollow thing through and he jumped out quick.

Winston the Weasel said that he doesn't think he would like to live in the hollow thing, so he won't go back in.

But he'll probably forget he said that
and go back again anyway.
He's so cute!

Lovelyn

Missa The Mouse

Moon and Stars

Don't you love it when the stars stop changing? I do! I love it when the stars are changing too, but when they stop, some of my favorite smells happen!

And the animals come out to play more too. And so does the wind! It has to shake the trees so they will wake up and grow their leaves again.

The little baby animals come out too. They are so cute! Ha Ha! I just want to hug and kiss all of them! And mostly I do, but I have to be careful with the baby skunks though. Really careful.

Have you ever watched baby rabbits? They are so funny to watch! They will be sitting next to their mother and eating clover, (which tastes good by the way), and then they act like they got hit by a sky bright and they jump way up and their legs start kicking everywhere and when they hit the ground again they are already running! Haa Haa!!

Then they run so fast they fall over or run into something, like a rock. Then they just stop and start eating again like nothing happened at all.

And they are so cute,

I just have to kiss them!

I love rabbits.

Remember the mice that live in the hollow thing? We thought the animal thing ate them but it didn't.

One of them doesn't live in the hollow thing anymore.

I saw her down by the quick water getting a drink and I said, "Hello Missa the mouse, what are you doing outside the hollow thing?"

Missa the mouse is a really fun thing to call a mouse! Ha Ha! But what is really fun is to go into the woods when Septad the snake is around.

How is that for a fun name! Septad! Ha Ha! And I can call him that too because he thinks it sounds important.

I stand in the woods and yell, "Missa Mouse!" very loud and I hear Septad the snake yell, "Oh yes, I'm missing a mouse! I'm sure I had a mouse here but it appears to be missing now! So that mouse is probably mine! Hold onto it tight, don't let it go! I'll be right there!"

And he comes slithering fast to get the mouse. But I don't ever have one. And he says, "Hello Miss Lovelyn," (remember I said everybody calls me

Miss Lovelyn?) He says, "Hello Miss Lovelyn, oh, no mouse? It slipped away again? Too bad. Try to hold tighter next time, they make such good companions."

Haa Haa!! He says that a lot. That they make such good companions, but he probably just wants to eat them.

Anyway, Missa the mouse (Ha!) said that she didn't want to live in the hollow thing anymore.

I asked her why and Missa the mouse started talking very fast. All mice talk very fast. Sometimes I have to slow them down with Faerie magic to understand them.

She said, "Miss Lovelyn, (see), I just couldn't stay there anymore I was so frightened that the animal thing would make me fly again and I'm not a squirrel or bird or something that flies and I don't think..."

Missa the mouse talked on and on and on. Mice do that too. She told me a funny story though! Ha Ha!

She told me that after she had eaten the food that the animal thing always has for the mice, she was sleepy and wanted to find a nice warm place to sleep.

She said that she went behind the rock with the bent tree growing out of it but it wasn't hot. Remember the rock Winston the Weasel, (Ha! Winston the Weasel!), told me about? I'm surprised he remembered it, but he did.

Well, Missa the mouse, who isn't as tubby as she was when she lived in the hollow thing, said that she was so sleepy that she hadn't seen the animal thing curled up on the log that squishes down. But when she came out from behind the black rock Missa the mouse saw it there.

And she said that the animal thing looked so warm and cozy sleeping there she just wanted to curl up with it and sleep too.

Missa the mouse thought it would be alright because the animal thing hadn't even tried to eat any of the mice.

She said the animal thing had one of its paws laying open by its head and Missa the mouse thought that would be a good place to sleep so she wouldn't get squished if the animal thing rolled over.

So she climbed up the log and into the paw. She said it was warm and soft and curled to just the right size for her to sleep in and she snuggled into the paw and went to sleep.

Missa the mouse (A fun name for a mouse I think! Ha!) said she was having the best dreams when the animal thing moved and woke her up.

She opened her eyes and so did the animal thing and they just stared at each other.

Then the animal thing made a really fun loud screechy noise, better than any of the other ones it made before, and then, Missa the mouse told me, it made her fly!

I have seen a horse fly, but I have never seen a mouse fly! Haa Haa!

She said even though she was flying upside down she could see the animal thing running around and jumping up and down shaking its paws and screeching!! Haa Haa!!

I wish I saw that! Ha! Ha!

Anyway when Missa the Mouse hit the ground, she waddled out of the hollow thing as fast as she could. (Remember all the mice got tubby?)

And now she won't go back.

Missa the mouse said she really misses the food and hot rock though.

But she doesn't want to fly again.

Lovelyn

Ephraheen The Eagle

Sun and Sky with Wind

Lovelyn again, La Ti Da!
Remember I said the wind has to wake
up the trees? Well it is here!
I love the wind.
It makes the trees bend and sway and
move a lot to wake them up. I watch with
Faerie sight to see inside the trees.
There is water in the trees that has to move
so the trees can grow leaves, and the wind
wakes up the water when it makes the trees
bend and sway.

Trees can be very grumpy when they wake up too! Ha Ha! If they get too grumpy they throw sticks and branches! Ha!

But after they wake up they are mostly friendly though.

If you ever want to know a secret ask the wind. It knows lots of secrets. And it will tell you too. Not secrets from here, but secrets from someplace else.

I have never been to someplace else, but that is where the wind says the secrets come from.

When the wind is waking up the trees I like to fly to the top and hold on tight and ride the tree in the wind! That's fun!

Remember I saw Filbert the flying squirrel (who is mostly Filbert the walking squirrel now) go past! He is so funny!

When I was up in the tree and the wind was resting I saw Edward the eagle. Not a very good name for an Eagle I don't think. But that is what he calls himself so that's what he is.

It is hard to think of a fun name for an Eagle. I don't know why, but it is. Ha! That makes me laugh!

Well I saw Edward the eagle, (who I will find a fun name for), flying high in the sky and then diving straight down at the deep water very fast and then flying straight up into the sky.

He kept doing that. I couldn't see the deep water so I looked with Faerie sight and saw Drucilla the duck. Ha! That is a really good name for a duck! And I can call her that too because mostly her head is under water and she can't hear me anyway.

Ducks are so funny when they eat. Their heads go down and their tails go up and their little duck feet start kicking and splashing! Haa Haa!!

I tried to eat upside down like that but I got dizzy. But ducks don't mind. I think they like being dizzy. Ha Ha!

Anyway, Edward the eagle, (Maybe Ephraheen the Eagle. That's a big name

for an Eagle. (Ha!), was diving straight
down at Drucilla the duck.

Drucilla the duck saw him and swam
down into the deep water and Edward
the eagle, (maybe Ephraheen), would fly
straight up into the sky. Drucilla the
duck would pop up and swim in circles

like a dizzy duck. Ha Ha! A dizzy duck! And she would be laughing. Ducks laugh really funny!

Edward the eagle would fly straight at her, then she would swim under the deep water. They kept doing that.

I guess Edward the eagle got tired because he sat on a stump in the deep water. But he kept watching Drucilla swim though.

He flew very close to the deep water straight at Drucilla the duck, but she saw him and swam down into the deep water.

Edward the eagle flew back to the stump to rest. Drucilla the duck popped up and off he went straight at her. She swam into the thick bushes and he started to fly home.

Drucilla the duck was laughing. That really does sound funny! Ha Ha! I hope you hear a duck laugh!

Anyway I flew over to him and said, "Hello Edward the eagle!"

And he said, "Oh, hello Miss Lovelyn."

But he didn't sound too happy.

I said, "Can I call you Ephraheen the eagle instead of Edward the eagle? I think it sounds more Eagley, don't you?"

And he said, kind of grumpy, "Oh I don't care, call me what you like."

And I said, "Ok, Ephraheen the eagle!" (I think that's much better, don't you?"). I asked him what he was doing with Drucilla the duck.

He said, "That's a little game we play. I try to ask her to come back to my nest so I can give her fish, and she swims down into the deep water."

He sounded _very_ grumpy when he said that.

Eagles can be like that.

Kind of tricky.

He said he wanted to give her fish, but he probably just wanted to eat her.

Lovelyn

Seymore The Snapping Turtle

Moon Bright

The quick water is singing and dancing with the moon. It is so pretty I watch and listen and sing and dance too!

We don't sing words though, just pretty sounds and we twirl and fly and splash! Ha Ha! And laugh too!

The quick water gets very excited when the stars stop changing and it wakes up again.

I saw Brimley the bear, (my favorite

bear), he said, "Hello Miss Lovelyn. I heard you singing with the quick water. That is very nice to wake up to."

And then he gave me a hug. He is so sweet! I love Brimley the bear.

He doesn't get excited about much though. He is kind of calm and steady mostly. Unless he sees a honey tree or a hillside of blueberries!

Then his eyes get sparkly and he makes low grumbly yummy noises. Haa Haa! But he doesn't jump up and down when he gets excited like the chipmunks do.

They can get very excited! And they get excited about almost anything! Ha! And they will run around telling everybody they see about it. And whatever happened gets bigger and bigger too!

Charley the chipmunk Ha! (a good name for a chipmunk I think), had a leaf fall on his head and he got very excited.

He screeched in his little Charley the chipmunk voice and ran all over the woods telling the story.

He said a leaf landed on his head and how strange that a leaf had fallen from the very top of a tree and landed right on his head. Then he said that the tree must have done it on purpose because it couldn't have just have happened that way.

Then it was a twig that landed on his head,
then a stick, then a branch,
then a limb. Ha Ha!!

Then he said the biggest tree in the forest
laid down right on top of his little Charley
the chipmunk head! But he is so strong, he
said, that he just pushed that big old tree
right back up and fixed it so it wouldn't
lay down again and you can't even tell that
it laid down anyway!

Chipmunks are really fun! But you
can't believe everything they say though.

You can believe turtles though, they
always tell the truth and they are smart too.

Seymore the snapping turtle, Ha Ha!
Seymore! I call him that because he

walks so slow he sees more along the way. Ha! Clever, don't you think?

And I can call him that too. He says he thinks it's ironic because he thinks he goes very fast!

His mouth is very fast, it has to be to catch fish to eat. But the rest of him is really slow.

He likes to know things too. He said he would run very, very fast close to the hollow thing to see if he could get a better look at the animal thing that lives there so he could know what it is.

Seymore the snapping turtle (ha ha!) says he can run so fast because his shell lets the wind slip right over it and it doesn't slow him down at all. He said, "Why Miss Lovelyn, I am probably the fastest runner in the forest."

I said, "What about the snails?"

And he said, "I just let them go past because I don't want them to think poorly of themselves." Haa Haa!!

He is always saying something smart like that.

He told me he was going to run as fast as he could just in case the animal thing came out of the hollow thing and it is some kind of Moose. I still don't think it is a Moose, but it is crazy anyway.

I told him I wanted to watch

and he said, "You can watch Miss Lovelyn, but don't try to keep up with me. I don't want you to hurt your wings trying to fly that fast. Just watch with Faerie sight and you'll be alright."

He makes me smile so much.

He is so serious.

I told him I would fly high to the top of a tree and dance with the wind and watch from there.

Seymore the snapping turtle, (which is a lot to say, but fun just the same! Ha!), said "Now don't look away or you might miss my run. I may need you to say what happens because I will be going so fast."

I said I would watch very close.

When moon and stars and sun and sky said hello, Seymore the snapping turtle started running like a Pine Martin!

If the Pine Martin was still sleeping anyway! Ha!

I did watch with Faerie sight and Seymore the snapping turtle squinted his little turtle eyes against the wind and ducked his little turtle head down a bit so he could go faster. Haa Haa Haa!!!

I almost fell out of the tree I was laughing so hard!

I watched and watched and watched. Then I fell asleep because the wind was singing a hushing song with the trees.

But I don't think I missed anything though, I woke up and Seymore the snapping turtle wasn't far along.

A butterfly landed on Seymore's shell and Seymore yelled, "Get off! Get off! At this speed the hard wind will snap you in two!"

The Butterfly, (whose name I don't know but will think of one for, maybe), looked around to see the hard wind. Then it  laughed and flew away. Ha Ha!

Butterfly laughs are very pretty, like a tinkling kind of music, almost like

Faerie music, but not quite
as pretty as that, of course.

I went to play with the quick water
and came back to watch Seymore the
snapping turtle, at no shadow.

I saw the animal thing looking out of
one of the openings in the hollow thing that
is covered with the strange ice
that won't melt.

It was showing its teeth and then
disappeared. Then the animal thing came
out of the hollow thing and started walking
slowly toward Seymore the snapping turtle.

Seymore saw the animal thing coming
and he squinted his little turtle eyes even
more and ducked his little turtle head

and grimaced with his little turtle mouth,
ha ha!! He was trying to go faster I guess,
but he couldn't.

The animal thing kept showing its teeth
and getting closer. Of course I thought it
was probably going to eat Seymore
but it didn't.

It was holding something in its paws
and it held it out to Seymore the snapping
turtle and the thing in the animal things
paws made sky bright like when there
is cover with water.

But it didn't make any sky booms at
all. Just sky bright.

I have seen sky bright smash a tree, but
this sky bright didn't hurt

Seymore the snapping turtle at all.
Maybe his shell was too hard to break.

Anyway, the animal thing gave
up trying to hit Seymore the snapping
turtle with sky bright and went back into
the hollow thing. And Seymore kept
running. Ha! Running!

I went to listen to the deep water. It
sings very low soothing sounds and it makes
me feel glowy and smooth. I feel like that
curled up with Brimley the bear when I
visit him when he sleeps too.

Sun and sky said hello to moon and
stars and I went to see Seymore the
snapping turtle. He was almost into the
woods and I waited in front of him to ask

what he thought the animal thing might be.

He got a little closer and started yelling and yelling, "Get out of the way! Get out of the way! I can't slow down!!"

I was thinking, no you can't slow down, if you go any slower you will be going backwards. Haa Haa!!

But I didn't say it.

He slowed down enough to stop and was breathing very hard.

He said, "Oh my, (breath breath) it is a good thing (breath breath) that you have Faerie magic Miss Lovelyn (breath breath) so you can get (breath breath) out of the way quickly. (breath breath)

I probably would have run right over you (breath breath) otherwise.

Haa Haa!! Ha! He is so serious, like I said! Ha ha!

I asked him what kind of animal the animal thing is and he said he didn't really get to look close enough to know. He said he should have slowed down but he had to run faster because the animal thing was throwing sky bright at him and he had to outrun it so he didn't get hit.

I asked if he would run past again and he said, (Ha!) "Oh no, too dangerous for the others, I could barely stop and I don't want to run somebody over you know."

I smile so much with him.

I don't know why the animal thing
didn't catch him.
Maybe it doesn't eat turtle.

Lovelyn

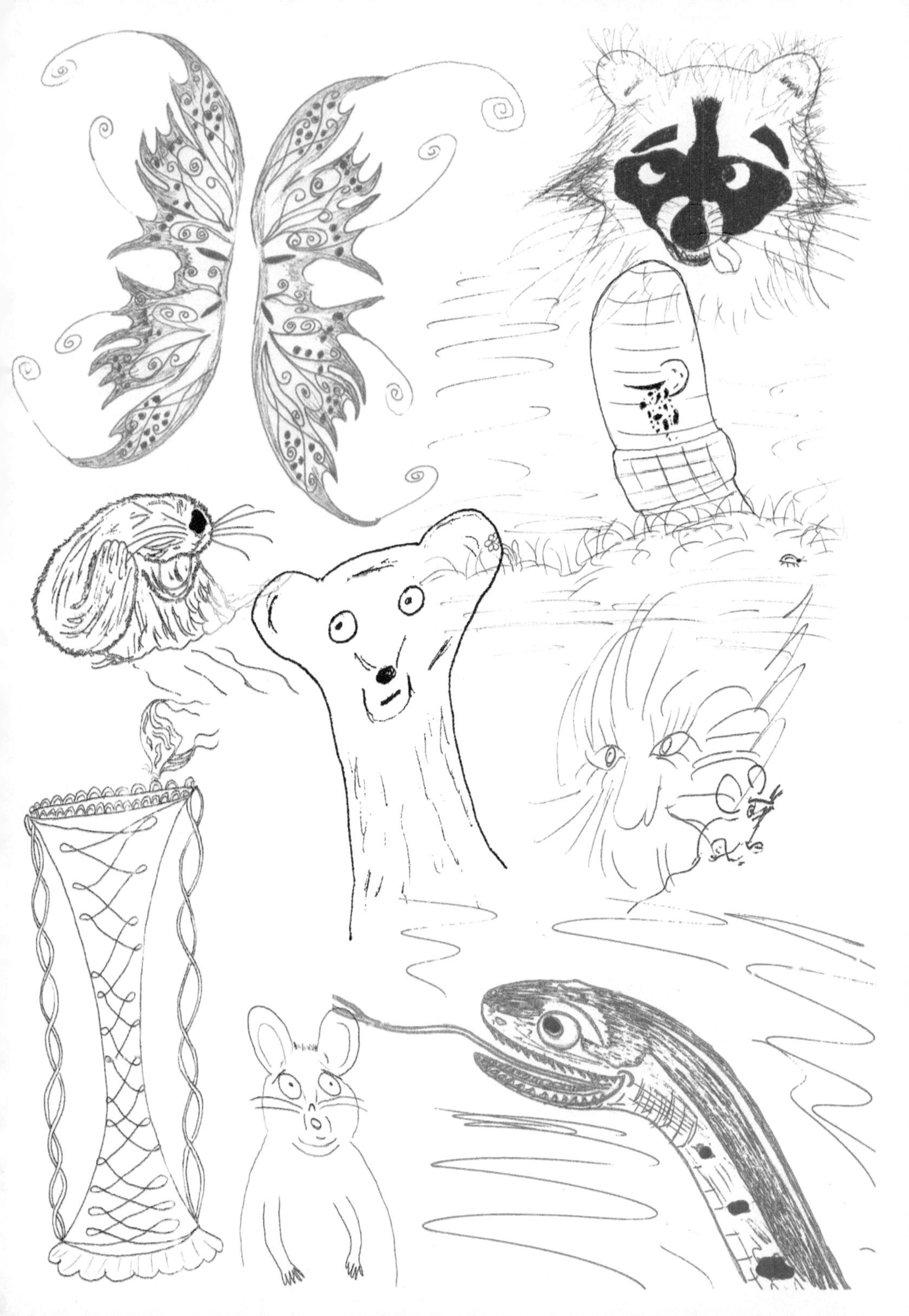

Hi, Derek here,

I just want to let you know that all of the tales that Lovelyn tells are based on the afore mentioned wild beasts running about, in the manner described, with some slight exaggeration perhaps on Lovelyn's part, (totally beyond my control), inside or around the hollow thing that I used to live in near Long Lake, NY.

If you have had wild beasts running about inside or around the hollow thing that you live in, excluding the children of course, and would like Lovelyn, possibly, to include the tale in an upcoming volume of "Diary of an Adirondack Faerie", please send a brief description of the incident to:

adkfaerie_lovelyn@yahoo.com

with the word "Lovelyn" in the subject line.

If your tale is used you will receive a free volume of the Diary in which your animal encounter is lied about...er... exaggerated...um, I mean described in a most honest and truthful fashion.

Thanks, I hope that you are having a smiling day!

Derek

www.ingramcontent.com/pod-product-compliance
Lightning Source LLC
Chambersburg PA
CBHW021025120726
47905CB00009B/3175